LOVE ALWAYS FINDS ITS WAY. IS IT?

HARSH PARMAR

Everyone who waited eagerly for this book, this is on you. Thank you to keep patience while this book was in progress.

Contents

Acknowledgements

Hi!

Thank you to all my readers for reading this book.

This book is not an effort of one person alone. I will get short of words if I express my gratitude to every single of them.

First of all, I would like to thank my parents who gave their support and encouraged me for writing.

Then I would like to offer my thanks to my friends for their invaluable support and time that they have given for the completion of this book. They were the ones who kept me involved in the book and continuously asked me about its progress.

I am also thankful to the entire team of Notion Press, who gave me the opportunity to publish my work so that it can reach millions of readers around the globe.

Last but not least, I once again thank my readers who chose my book over the others and found some time out of their busy schedule to read it.

Preface

Welcome!

The book will take you on a wonderful journey of friendship, love, anger, rejection and rebound.

The story revolves around a boy from Udaipur, named Sameer, who is studious but at the same time friendly. Love has never been his priority, but he also feels himself quite lonely. He is happy with his family and friends.

One day, a girl named Ishika, came and proposed to him. He accepted the proposal willingly and began his journey of love.

Sameer and Ishika along with their love life, also focused on their ambitions. Will they be able to make balance between ambitions and love? Or, will they have to leave one?

Read to find out.

Love always finds its way. Is it?

To love, lovers and their ambitions...

CHAPTER ONE

Sameer arrived at the station of Udaipur from his college to spend the winter holidays with his family and friends. Just when he stepped out of the station, his phone rang. It was from his father to know about his whereabouts. He answered the call and informed him that he is on his way home. A taxi stopped by, he stepped in and left for home.

On the way, he received a conference call from his friends - Rohit, Siya, and Jayesh. They were excited to meet Sameer after a long time. They invited Sameer to come to Fateh Sagar Lake at 10 at night. They will be waiting there. Sameer agreed. He too was excited to meet his friends.

When he reached home, he was surprised to find his friends there. They all hugged Sameer when they got sight of him. Sameer went in and touched his parents' feet to take their blessings. They blessed him with "Jug Jug Jeeyo, beta", meaning 'long live my child'. Then he took a shower and they all sat at the dining table to have dinner. Sameer's mother had cooked paneer tadka, Peshawari Naan and Mava Kachori. All these dishes were Sameer's favorite. Sameer's taste buds came alive after eating so delicious homemade food. His friends enjoyed the food and thanked Sameer's mother for inviting them there. They all talked for a while. They were so lost in conversation that they lost track of time. Suddenly, Rohit's eyes fell on the wall clock. It was past 10:30 p.m. He insisted to everyone that they should leave for Fateh Sagar Lake now. Sameer and his friends stood up to leave. Everyone stepped inside Rohit's car. Siya sat beside Rohit. They were dating each other for the last two years. Sameer and Jayesh took the back seat. Rohit turned on the music and they left. The road was empty and quiet. They reached the lake enjoying the music and talking.

The atmosphere around the lake was calm and serene. The place was devoid of pollution. A mild breeze was blowing. Jayesh informed everyone that the lake was built by Maharaja Jai Singh but it was named after Maharaja Fateh Singh, who made a dam and enlarged the lake. The lake was surrounded by hills. Watching a sunset here is so blissful. Colorful lights illuminated the entire lake. As the boating hours had passed, many boats were tied to a corner. Everyone sat down on the stairs near the lake. Staring at the colorful water, Siya started the conversation.

"So, Sameer, how is your experience of returning after about six months?" She asked Sameer.

"Well, I feel like I am back in heaven. Seriously, there is no place like home." Sameer replied.

"Yes, you are right. By the way after how long have you come to this lake?" She asked again.

"Umm, after about 3 years. Last I came here with my cousins. We had such a blast that day, we did boating and had a picnic. One of my cousins accidentally fell into the lake while boating. Luckily, she knew how to swim." Sameer shared his experience.

"Wow, looks like you enjoyed too much that day."

"Yup."

Siya now turned to Rohit.

"Rohit, when was the last time you brought me here?" Siya asked Rohit.

"I don't remember. I am sorry."

"You are so oblivious. You don't remember anything. Do you remember me or you have forgotten who I am?" Siya became angry.

"I am sorry, Siya. I will never forget you. I promise. Please don't be angry." Rohit tried to calm her down.

"No. Stay away from me. I don't want to talk to you." Siya started crying.

"Siya, please stop crying. I promise I will always be with you."

"Siya, don't cry. What's the big deal if Rohit forgot one thing. You should be thankful that he is committed to you. He will always be there for you." Sameer insisted.

"But he forgets everything. He even forgot the day he proposed to me." Siya relucted.

"Rohit, that's your mistake. How can you be so ignorant? Say sorry to her and from now on try to remember the small moments that you two cherish together." Sameer advised Rohit.

"Ok, fine. I accept my mistake, Siya. Please forgive me. It will not happen again. Rohit apologized to Siya.

"Apology accepted," Siya said.

Rohit hugged Siya tightly. They embraced each other for several minutes. They were lost in the serene atmosphere of the lake. Sameer and Jayesh brought them back to the present moment by teasing them that "Guys, save something for upcoming days." Rohit and Siya started laughing with Sameer and Jayesh.

It was a reunion after a very long time. Everyone shared their stories and experiences and they talked until dawn. Then, they all went to their respective homes to get some sleep.

CHAPTER TWO

It was New Year's Eve. Rohit had thrown a grand party at one of the luxurious hotels of the city. At the hall entrance, two men dressed as royal guards were standing to welcome the guests. The banquet hall of the hotel was decorated with various flowers, balloons, decorative stars, decorative lamps, fairy lights, and garlands. Various food items including starters, delicious cuisine, and desserts were there. The food stalls were crowded with people. Next to the banquet hall was a garden. The garden soil was filled with green grass. The whole garden was illuminated using decorative lights. Different flowers in the garden spread their sweet aroma which made the evening even more blissful. A mild breeze spread the floral smell all around the garden and in the banquet hall. A band was playing and singing various songs.

Rohit and Jayesh were waiting in the garden for Sameer and Siya with a mocktail in hand. It was getting a little late, so, Rohit took out his phone to call Sameer. Just when he was about to call, a message popped up from Sameer. It said that Sameer and Siya are stuck in traffic, so it would take about half an hour to reach the party. Rohit replied with "Ok" and went inside the hall with Jayesh to meet the guests. Guests praised Rohit for organizing such a wonderful party. They praised the decoration and the food. Some insisted that Rohit should organize such a party every year. Rohit thanked everyone for their appraisal. He and Jayesh then went to the stall of rabdi maal pua, a famous dessert of Udaipur to pass the time while waiting for Sameer and Siya.

Finally, Sameer arrived with Siya. Siya was looking glamorous in her pinkish-purple gown. Seeing them, Rohit rushed towards them. He kissed Siya and told Sameer that he should have left home a little early as this was the time fixed for traffic.

"I left on time but your girlfriend takes too much time to get ready," Sameer replied.

"Yes, girls need to look best to grab attention. So, they need time to get ready." Siya said.

"You should grab my attention only, not others'," Rohit said to Siya.

"Shut up, you jealous," Siya said.

"It's too noisy here. Let's take a mocktail and move out in the garden." Sameer said.

So, everyone grabbed a mocktail and headed towards the garden. They grabbed one of the tables arranged in the garden. Rohit raised a toast for the party being so amazing. They were laughing and talking and enjoying the evening.

"Sameer and Jayesh, don't you guys think that you should have a girlfriend?" Siya asked.

"I had one a while back," Jayesh answered.

"Then what happened?" Siya enquired.

"That relationship worked well for a few months. But after that, she started to try to rule over me. She had a problem with my every choice and action. From what I wear to what I eat, to whom I talk to what I do, she wanted to control everything. And I hate someone controlling my life, so I broke up with her."

"That's so tragic. I am feeling sorry for you, Jayesh." Siya said sympathetically.

"What about you, Sameer?" Siya turned to Sameer.

"To be honest, I never thought about it. My whole life I thought only about my career. Love has never been my priority. Maybe, someday, a girl will find me interesting and come to me and ask 'would you like to spend the rest of your life with me'."

"That's kind of attitude but romantic also," Siya said laughing.

"Now Siya, if you are done with your questions, can we have dinner?" Rohit interrupted.

"You are always hungry, Rohit. Why don't you get a job in some food industry?"

"Stop teasing me. It's not my fault that I am hungry."

"Ok, fine. Let's eat."

So, everyone grabbed their plates and went to the food corner. They filled their plates with different types of cuisines, and dessert and went to a table. They all praised the food. The food was very delicious.

After dinner, people started to leave. When there weren't many people in the garden, Rohit and Siya got some time together. After having some romantic chit-chat they hugged and kissed each other before leaving. Then, Rohit, Jayesh, Sameer, and Siya left. Rohit dropped Siya at her home. Sameer and Jayesh went together. Everyone thanked Rohit for throwing such an amazing and fun-filled party.

CHAPTER THREE

Sameer was enjoying his winter holidays. Catching up with friends, going to movies, spending time with parents, and enjoying the delicacies at home made him feel contented.

It was 1st January. Sameer had come late last night from Rohit's party, so, he was still asleep. The clock was about to hit 1 p.m. His mother, furious with her son's sleeping habit, entered Sameer's room to wake him up. Nice, warm winter sunlight was falling onto the bed where Sameer was sleeping. His mother snatched his blanket. No response came from Sameer. He was lost in his dream world. She shouted at him. Still, no response. She tried twice and thrice but Sameer wouldn't wake up. Fed up with the efforts, she came up with a handful of cold water and splashed it on Sameer's face. He woke up with a jolt.

"Mom. What are you doing? Let me sleep. It's so early." Sameer said in a sleepy voice.

"Early, you say. Look at the clock." His mother's voice was stern.

"What! It's 1:10 p.m," Sameer said shockingly looking at the clock.

"I don't understand why today's kids have to party till late at night. Party till morning and sleep till afternoon. That's all that today's generation does." His mother was angry.

"Sorry, mom. But it was a New Year Party." Sameer defended himself.

"So, does that mean you will sleep all day?"

"No, mom."

"Then, wake up, get a shower and come down for lunch. I have prepared your favorite food."

Listening that his favorite food was made, Sameer jumped up from his bed and immediately hurried to the bathroom for a shower. After the shower, he came running to the dining table to have lunch. His mother had prepared butter chicken, jeera rice, and moong dal halwa on the occasion of New Year. At the sight and aroma of a hot cooked meal, Sameer's mouth was filled with saliva. He couldn't wait to munch on the meal. His mother served the meal. Sameer ate, taking the best out of every bite. He was full up to his neck after lunch. He hugged his mother, telling her that the food was very delicious. His mother kissed his forehead and said, "I am glad you liked it. Now go and check your phone. Your friends have been calling you for the last 4 hours."

Sameer checked his phone. There were several messages and three missed calls from Rohit, five from Siya, and two from Jayesh. Sameer dialed Rohit's number. He picked up the call immediately.

"Where are you, bro?" asked Rohit.

"In the dreamland, bro," answered Sameer.

"Tell me, why did you call? Any plans for today?" asked Sameer.

"Yes, there is a plan but not for all of us. Siya and I haven't been on a date for several days. I thought I would take her for a movie and then dinner at a restaurant."

"That sounds great, Rohit. Enjoy your day. Make her happy and make sure that you don't make her cry like the last time when we met at Fateh Sagar Lake." Sameer warned Rohit.

"Yes, sure. But don't tell her. It's a surprise. Just tell her that I will pick her up at 4 o'clock from her house." said Rohit.

"Ok," Sameer responded.

"By the way, what about you? How will you spend the entire day?" asked Rohit.

"I will just sit back on the couch and binge on Netflix. Maybe, I will call Jayesh to give me company."

"Nice bro. Bye."

"Bye."

Sameer ended the call and called Siya.

"Hi, Sameer." She answered the call.

"Hello!" replied Sameer.

"Why didn't you pick up my call? I called you so many times."

"Sorry, Siya. I was sleeping. Mom had to wake me up."

"You are seriously lazy."

"I know I am."

"What are you doing today?"

"Sitting on the couch and streaming Netflix."

"Great. Anyway, have you heard from Rohit? Where is he? He hasn't called me all day. I am going to scream at him when he calls." Siya was annoyed.

"Siya, I have something to tell you."

"What is it?"

"Rohit has planned a surprise for you. He will pick you up from your house at 4 o'clock."

"What? Are you kidding? He and surprise are not perfect partners."

"Come on, Siya. Don't be so distrustful."

"Ok. Ok. I will see what he has planned."

"Good. Now go and get ready. It's close to 4."

"You are so kind, Sameer. Any girl would be lucky to have you in her life."

"Only if that day comes."

"Oh, Sameer. Don't be so disheartened. You will find your love."

"Let's see when that happens."

"Don't worry. I will help."

"Ok, Siya. Now go or you will be late."

"Sorry, Sameer. I have to hang up. And thanks for reminding me."

"Welcome. Now go. Bye."

"Bye, Sameer."

Then Sameer called Jayesh.

"Hey, Jayesh. What's up?

"Nothing bro. Only sleeping."

"Any plans for today?"

"None."

"Then, get ready and come to my place."

"Why?"

"We will spend the evening streaming Netflix."

"No, bro. Let me sleep."

"Come on, dude. You are lazier than me."

"Ok, fine. I will be there in an hour."

"Great. Bye."

"Bye."

At around 5 in the evening, Sameer's doorbell rang. It was Jayesh. Sameer welcomed him with a firm handshake and let him in. He requested his mother to arrange some snacks for them. Sameer took Jayesh to his room. He turned on his home theatre and switched on the TV and opened Netflix on it.

"What would you like to watch, Jayesh? Romance, action, mystery, or horror?" Sameer asked.

"Bro, romance is for lovers, I am afraid of ghosts and mystery is not something my brain can comprehend. So, I would better watch the action."

"Hmm... you are right. Romance is not for singles like us. But, why are you afraid of ghosts? They are not real."

"I don't know. I am just afraid."

"Ok. Let's see, what's there in action."

After much scrolling, they finally agreed on Assassin's Creed. Meanwhile, the snacks arrived. Sameer's mother had prepared veg pakoda with chilli chutney. Jayesh's mouth became watery from the smell. He immediately grabbed a handful of pakodas and got back on the couch to enjoy the movie. The sound of the home theatre made the movie even more thrilling to watch.

The movie is a video game adaptation. It is a sci-fi action film. The movie is about a guy called Callum Lynch, who through revolutionary technology unlocks his genetic memories, experiences, and the adventures of his ancestor, Aguilar de Nerha in 15th century Spain. Callum discovers, that he has descended from a mysterious secret society. The Assassins amasses incredible knowledge and skills to take on the oppressive and powerful Templar organization in the present day.

It was a 1 hour 55 minutes long movie which ended around 8 p.m. After watching the movie, both of them were hungry. They ordered chole-kulche and cold drinks from a restaurant through an online food delivery application. The food arrived within 30 minutes. They both started to munch on it as soon as the packet was opened. The food was so delicious that they started to snatch from each other's plates as small kids do. At last, the food was over, and with that, their fight ended. Then, they had cold drinks. Finally, their stomachs were satisfied. Jayesh then left for his home wishing Sameer and his parents good night.

That night, when Sameer was about to fall asleep, his cell phone rang. It was a conference call from Rohit and Siya. He rubbed his eyes and answered the call.

"Hello!" said Sameer in a sleepy voice.

"Hi! Sameer," said Siya cheerfully.

"Were you asleep?" asked Rohit.

"Yes," replied Sameer.

"Wake up now," said Siya.

"Why? What happened?" asked Sameer.

"Bro, so many things happened," said Rohit in excitement.

"You were right, Sameer. Rohit gave me the best surprise ever." Siya said expressing her happiness.

"What was the surprise?" asked Sameer.

"Rohit, you keep quiet. I'll tell him," said Siya.

"Listen, Sameer." said Siya.

"I am listening. You go on," said Sameer.

"First, he picked me up from my house and took me for a romantic movie. Then, we went for a walk in a nearby park. The atmosphere of the park was quite cold and euphoric. After that, he took me to a restaurant for candle-light dinner. Just when we finished dinner, Rohit was on one of his knees. From his back pocket, he took out a red box and opened it in front of me. There was a diamond ring inside. I couldn't believe my eyes at that moment. Was that happening for real? Yes, that was. My mouth fell open. He proposed to me for marriage and knowing that I delightedly accepted his proposal, he kissed me in front of everyone. People in the restaurant were watching us. But who cares about them when your stupid boyfriend proposes to you for marriage."

"Hey, I am not stupid." interfered Rohit.

"Yes, you are mister. Now keep quiet," said Siya.

"Wow! Congratulations to both of you. Well done, Rohit. So, when will be your wedding?" responded Sameer.

"Don't know. First, we have to convince our parents. They should get to know each other. Then, we will decide the date." said Siya.

"Great. I wish you two good luck," said Sameer.

"Thank you, bro," said Rohit.

"Thank you, Sameer," said Siya.

"Ok guys. Enjoy and embrace your bright future ahead," said Sameer.

"Ok Sameer, you must be feeling sleepy. Sorry to disturb you and thank you for listening. You can sleep now. Good night." said Rohit.

"Good night both of you," said Sameer.

"Good night," said Siya.

CHAPTER FOUR

The next day, Rohit messaged everyone to gather at Fateh Sagar Lake at 9 p.m. He wanted to celebrate his marriage proposal to Siya with his friends. But he didn't mention it in the message. Jayesh also wasn't aware of this proposal.

At the lake, Rohit and Siya were waiting for Jayesh and Sameer half an hour before the decided time. They had brought cake and candles to celebrate this special moment. Around 9 p.m., Sameer and Jayesh arrived on their bikes. Siya and Rohit were busy enjoying the view of the lake in each other's company. So, they didn't notice them coming.

"Now we won't get noticed, Jayesh." Sameer teased Siya and Rohit.

Jayesh couldn't understand what Sameer was saying. Siya and Rohit turned back.

"Sorry, guys." Rohit apologized.

"Hi! Jayesh and Sameer." Siya said.

"Hello, both of you." Sameer and Jayesh said in unison.

"Sameer, could you tell me why did you tell previously that we won't get noticed now?" asked Jayesh.

"You will find out in a few minutes," Sameer answered.

Sameer once again congratulated Rohit and Siya. Rohit then took out the cake and arranged candles on it. Jayesh still could not understand what was happening. Siya informed him that Rohit proposed to her yesterday for marriage and they are planning to tie a knot soon. Jayesh was shocked for a second but wished them good luck. Siya lighted the candles and together with Rohit, holding his hand, made a wish that they get married without any difficulty from their parents' side and blew off the candles. They cut the cake. But who eats cake nowadays? The whole cake was wasted in putting on one another's faces. Rohit and Siya found some romance in licking cake from each other's faces. Seeing them, Sameer and Jayesh moved a bit away from them to give them privacy.

After having some conversation, they ordered food for themselves. Having dinner with friends beside a lake is so wonderful. After having dinner together, all four of them left for home.

Sameer was lying on his bed scrolling his Instagram. He was very happy for Rohit and Siya. Thinking about them, he was smiling. Suddenly, it came to his mind that he also wanted a relationship that will turn into marriage and last forever. He wanted to celebrate his birthday with her, have sweet and silly fights with her, console her and make her laugh whenever she is angry or sad, live every possible moment with her to the fullest, and take her for night walks with her hand in his, dance in the rain with her, accessorize her hair every day with a new bunch of flowers and hug and kiss her now and then. But, most importantly, he wanted to have her for a lifetime.

Recalling and thinking about all this made him feel lonely and he became sad. With grief of loneliness, he turned his phone on silent and went to sleep.

The next morning, he was woken up by his alarm. It was 8 o'clock. He checked his phone. There was a mail from his college that exams were going to start in a week. So, holidays will be cut short. He became panicked. He didn't study anything on a single day of his winter holidays. He just had fun with everyone and completely forgot about his studies. He decided that he will study the whole time now until he is at home. No more catching up with friends, no movies, no parties. Only studies.

He rushed to the bathroom to freshen up and get a quick shower. He had breakfast that was quite simple and usual. He then locked himself in his room and took his pile of books. He just sat there staring at books, thinking, which subject should he start with. Finally, he decided to start with his favorite one, 'Chemistry'.

For the next few days at home, Sameer completely indulged himself in his preparations for exams.

Eventually, his vacation came to an end. On the last day of his vacation, Sameer went to meet his friends. They all ate together, had fun, hugged each other, and bade goodbye to Sameer. Rohit proudly and delightedly announced that his and Siya's parents have been convinced and are ready to let their children marry their choice. He informed Sameer and Jayesh that the wedding date will be decided soon and they are pre-invited. Sameer and Jayesh congratulated Rohit and Siya. And after that, Sameer left for home because he had to catch his train to Dehradun.

Before leaving for Dehradun, Sameer took blessings from his parents. His father presented him with a gift and blessed him to excel in his forthcoming exam. Then, he bade them goodbye and left.

CHAPTER FIVE

Sameer was back at his hostel. Exams were to commence in two days. So, he invested his whole time in his books.

He studied very hard. His exams started. With full hope and confidence, he appeared for all his exams and did well. On the last day of his exam, the college dean announced that the college is organizing an educational trip to Soham Himalayan Centre, Mussoorie. It would be a 2-days trip with accommodation and fooding provided by the college management. Students have to bear their travel charges. Seniors and juniors would go together on this trip. College buses would be available for taking them to and back from Mussoorie.

On the date decided, everyone boarded the college bus for the educational trip. During the journey, they were singing and played various games to pass the time.

Finally, they reached their lodging destination in Mussoorie. Everyone got off the bus and went to their allotted rooms to freshen up and get rest.

The first day of the trip was spent resting and enjoying the evening.

On the second day, they went to Soham Himalayan Centre. It is a museum in Mussoorie that showcases 'Himalayan-ness' with a variety of paintings, artifacts, etc.

with the commitment to preserve and promote it. It comprises Soham Hill Mart, the commercial wing, which is into design, production, and sale of arts. Also, the Sri Chamunda Peeth Temple, the center for meditation and religious worship. The Soham Himalayan Museum forms the core and is the center of attraction. The museum showcases paintings, murals, sculptures, artifacts, etc. Paintings, jewelry, utensils, etc. provide a piece of great knowledge about the Himalayan cultures and traditions.

While everyone was in the paintings section including Sameer, a girl approached him and led him to a quiet place, away from everyone. He had never seen her and had no idea who she was. She was beautiful and elegant. Sameer fell in love with her at first sight. She introduced herself that she is his junior and her name is Ishika. She was observing him and trying to talk to him for many days. Then, she knelt before him and proposed to him. Sameer couldn't take in what was happening. It was all too sudden for him. After catching a breath, he held her by her shoulder and got her up. She kissed him. Sameer held her hand and accepted her proposal. At this moment, Sameer remembered Siya's words. She had told him that one day he will find his love. And now, her words finally came to be true. Sameer was filled with hope.

Hearing someone's voice from a distance, they got aware of the surroundings and headed their way back to join everyone. On the way, they exchanged their phone numbers and talked about where they were from. Sameer was stunned to find that Ishika was also from Udaipur. He was filled with joy. Besides, it was a relief for them that no one noticed their short escape and rejoin.

Professors of the college and a local guide were informing and explaining to students about various things.

Students were also curious and enthusiastic. They showed a keen interest in learning new things, cultures, and traditions.

But Sameer and Ishika were busy with each other. None of them were listening to what the professors and guides were explaining. They were preoccupied discussing their life and knowing each other more and more.

This is what happens when you fall in love with someone. Nothing around you matters but the person. You can't stop listening to your partner. You wouldn't want to take your eyes off of them. Love changes us for real. No matter how hard you resist, you will start getting attracted to them beyond your imagination.

The tour of Soham Himalayan Centre was finally concluded and everyone returned to where they were staying. The next day, they had to leave.

Sameer and Ishika hugged each other. Unwillingly, they too had to go to their respective rooms.

Sameer was happy like never before. He couldn't sleep that night in excitement. He checked the time on his phone. It showed 2:09 a.m. He felt the desperation to call Ishika, but tried to control it and tossed his phone aside. For the next half an hour, he kept turning from right to left, left to right, and again. But sleep was nowhere near him. At last, he could no more control his excitement and desperation and reached for his phone to dial her number. No answer on the first ring. He called again. Ishika picked up this time and in a sleepy voice, she said, "Hello."

Sameer in his excitement, said, "Wake up. I am not feeling sleepy. Talk to me for some time."

Ishika on the other side, still in sleep, said, “Not now Sameer. Please let me sleep and you too go and get some sleep. We have to return tomorrow. Good night.”

Sameer frowned. With his excitement blown up, Sameer said, “I will try. Good night” and ended the call.

The whole night, Sameer tried to fall asleep but couldn’t. He was lost in her thoughts. How she proposed to him; how he fell in love with her when he saw her for the first time; his first kiss and also Siya’s words–were all running through his mind. Ishika was in his every thought.

When you don’t expect anything and that happens, the excitement of it doesn’t let you sleep. The whole incident keeps playing through your brain without a pause. At this moment, sleep gets nowhere near you.

Sameer was still trying to get away from his thoughts and get some sleep when the sun made its appearance. The morning yellow light peeped through the window disrupting his effort even more. There was hustle and bustle everywhere to board the bus. Tired of trying, Sameer gave up; got up from his bed; packed his belongings, and got ready.

Everyone boarded the bus and was on their way back to Dehradun.

CHAPTER SIX

Sameer started his day with the thought of Ishika. He spent his entire morning routine thinking about her. In between lecture breaks, he used to write a few lines or verses that he would recite to her at night on phone calls. After class lectures, they would catch up near a tea stall outside their college. At night, he talked with her for hours on phone. This had become his daily life now.

They both were happy and contented with their relationship. Ishika was an ambitious girl. She wanted to become a singer and she was so good at singing. She used to participate in cultural programs and competitions held in college. Also, she always secured either a 1st or 2nd position every time. Never 3rd.

However, her father hated singers. He thought that songs are one the biggest reasons people lose track and end up broken. He thought, songs don't let people concentrate; they are just a waste of time. He was against her daughter's dream of becoming a singer. She had to hide from her father's ears whenever she had to practice. Twice or thrice, her father got to listen to her singing. He got furious and in aggression and hatred, he beat her up with a bamboo stick, locked her up in a storeroom, and restricted her from food.

Instead of suffering from so much pain and torment, she never gave up on her dream. She always tried for one chance. If she gets it, she would leave her family for her dream.

Sometimes, she cried in front of Sameer telling him all this. Sameer would think that when he settles down, he would try everything in his reach to make Ishika a successful singer. But he never told her about this thought.

Ishika started imagining Sameer as her 'man of dreams' with whom she can always be comfortable, feel secure, and spend her life.

Sameer never thought about marrying Ishika or any other girl. He first wanted to earn for himself and later think about marriage. But he loved Ishika very much. Though the idea of marrying her never came to his mind, somewhere, deep inside, he too wanted to spend his life with her.

Sameer also had a dream of his own. He wanted to become an artist and open an Art & Craft Institution. But he did not have enough money to do that currently. So, he had decided to first pursue a career in his field of study, earn and save some money and then invest in his dream.

Both of them had their vision and dream in mind which was their priority. They decided to support each other in achieving one another's dreams and let marriage wait until then.

CHAPTER SEVEN

One afternoon, Sameer and Ishika were sitting in the college playground during lunch break. Killing their mood, Sameer's phone rang. He took it out of the pocket to find it was Siya. Ishika asked him who the caller is. Sameer informed her it was Siya and attended the call.

"How are you, Sameer?" asked Siya.

"I am fine. Tell about you," replied Sameer.

"I am good. Your voice seems different today. It is energetic. It is hopeful. May I know the reason behind it?"

"Oh Siya, there is no reason in particular. It's just that I came back from our college trip a few days back. And so, I am feeling quite free and calm." Sameer lied. The real reason was Ishika.

"Well then, I have good news for you."

"What? Let me guess. You have decided your wedding date."

"Right guess. It is on 14th February."

"Awesome date for a memorable occasion. But that's nearly 10 days from now."

"Would you be able to come?"

"Yes. Definitely."

"Great. Let me inform Jayesh also. Need to go. Bye."

"Bye."

After ending the call, Sameer noticed that Ishika wasn't there. He looked all around him, but she was nowhere to be found. He thought she must be feeling hungry, so she might have gone to the canteen. He went there, but to his surprise, she wasn't there. He called her. But she rejected the call. Sameer reached the classroom looking for her. He found her sitting alone with her head hidden down at the back of the classroom. He walked up to her only to find that she was crying. He asked her why was she crying. She didn't tell him anything. He insisted again. But she didn't want to speak. Sameer sat there for some time. Finally, she spoke. The reason behind her tears was Sameer talking to a girl other than her and that too so cheerfully. This made her jealous and hurt her. So, she left him talking there with Siya without even a word.

Sameer sighed. He tried to explain to her that she is just a friend and she called to inform him about her wedding. But Ishika wasn't ready to listen. He kept consoling her, but she asked him to leave her alone and she left. Sameer sat there putting a hand on his forehead.

In the evening, Ishika called Sameer and apologized for her behavior. Sameer told her that it is alright, but next time, she should listen to him before judging anything. He convinced her that he is committed to her. He doesn't even sneak up on other girls. So, she should never doubt him. Ishika realized her mistake and promised, she would talk to him before she thinks anything wrong about him.

This was their first fight. Sameer had an intuition that there will be many more in the future. He was worried about how he would handle her anger this intense. Another fear struck him, what if she decides to leave him someday in anger? What if he is not able to calm her down when she is mad at him? For once, he started to curse the educational trip. If there had not been any trip, he wouldn't have to worry about such things. For once, he wanted to break up with her but at the same time, he realized that he cannot live without her and wanted her for his whole life.

Fear, worry, and affection surrounded him and his thoughts. Ishika again called him. He was in no mood of talking to anyone, so he didn't answer. She called again. This time, he declined the call and turned off his phone. She called for the third time. This time, the recorded voice said that the phone is switched off. She understood Sameer must be tensed and sad with her behavior today. So, she thought to give him some space.

The next day, they met after the class. Sameer tried his best to hide his tension and sadness. But Ishika sensed it by his face. She kissed him. He didn't kiss her back. Ishika understood how badly he was hurt by her behavior. In trying to cheer up his mood, she spilled something stupid out of her lips. She told him that she will get mad at him like this at times and that she loves being consoled by him and he is going to regret forever about this relationship for this reason his whole life. This added fuel to the fire inside Sameer's heart. Though Ishika had no bad intention about what she said but it hurt Sameer even more. She tried making up for this, but he immediately left, moving her aside.

Repenting her words, Ishika left and cried for hours alone in her room.

Later that night, Sameer called her. Ishika said sorry. Her voice was still low. Sameer guessed she must have cried.

He didn't want this fight to continue any longer. So, he consoled her, saying, not to tell things like this again. Ishika promised, she would never talk like this again.

Thus, with that, their first fight finally came to its end.

Sameer felt relieved. But he was still worried about the future. The thought of future fights took a toll on him. Wondering how he will handle her next time, he fell asleep.

CHAPTER EIGHT

It was a bright pleasant day. Sun was quite a bit warm. The ground was covered with lush green grass. Beautiful, bright, and colorful flowers were fluttering in the wind, spreading their sweet smell everywhere around. Birds were chirping, singing in their voice in the sky. At a distance, was a tree with vast branches and shadow underneath it. There, sat Ishika. Sameer was lying on his back, resting his head on her lap. Ishika was stroking her fingers through Sameer's hair. Sameer was staring at Ishika's face, which glowed in the bright yellow sunlight. Her shiny brown eyes showered her love for him. Sameer moved his hand up, running from her waist to her shoulder, feeling every inch of her. At her shoulder, his hand stopped. He got up and moved his other hand to her other shoulder. He turned her towards him. His right hand was slowly moving towards her face. His palm brushed against her cheeks. His thumb brushed her lips. She shivered at his touch on her lips. Both of his hands were on her cheeks. They were looking into each other's eyes. Their eyes showed how deeply they are in love. Sameer moved his head closer to Ishika's. So close, that she could feel his warm breath touching her face. She closed her eyes feeling his breath even more. Sameer's lips touched Ishika's. The feel of her moist lips was overwhelmingly pleasurable. And they kissed. They kissed and kissed and kissed for the next few minutes. It seemed that they haven't kissed for ages. None of them wanted to stop. The desire to feel each other took total control over them. They were completely immersed in each other. But then, Sameer's phone alarm rang.

Sameer woke up in dismay. *Why the alarm has to ring at such wonderful moments?* He wondered. His romantic dream was left halfway. Irritated, he grabbed his phone and thrashed it on the floor. He tried to go back to sleep. But his effort was in vain. He woke up, walked up to where his phone was lying thrashed, lifted it, and checked it. It had gone off and its screen was cracked due to the impact with the floor. He turned it on. The phone screen lit up. It got no harm inside. He breathed a sigh of relief.

Sameer then went to the bathroom to get ready for his class. He couldn't pay attention to his class either. From the time he woke, his dream kept revolving in his mind. He was still annoyed with the alarm. The kiss felt so real even in his dream that he could feel her lips on his even now. His dream indeed left its mark on him.

After the class, Sameer met Ishika and told her about his dream. He also told her, how it was broken by the stupid alarm and how he was feeling about it all day.

Listening to Sameer's dream was left incomplete, and she started laughing. Sameer looked at her and frowned. He couldn't understand what was funny about it. She stopped laughing when she saw Sameer's frowned face.

"I didn't know you are so romantic, Mr. Senior." She commented.

She didn't see any expression on his face. She repeated it but gripping his cheeks with her fingers and moving his face to and fro this time.

"Okay-okay, that's alright," Sameer told, releasing her grip.

"Let's go for a walk." She told him.

"Will that cheer me up?" He asked.

"Of course. I have a surprise for you." She sounded convincing.

Sameer agreed and they headed out of the college campus towards a street that wasn't used too often by people. They walked quite a distance holding hands. After walking to some distance, Ishika stopped Sameer. She was staring into his glistening eyes. His eyes were filled with surprise. Ishika pulled his face towards her by clenching his shirt. She touched her lips to his and kissed him. This was a passionate kiss, just like the one Sameer had dreamed of. Sameer lifted her in his arms and hugged her intensely.

It started to get dark. They realized they have to go back. Sameer kissed her again and they were on their way back.

"So did you like the surprise?" Ishika asked on the way back.

"Liked? I enjoyed it overjoyfully. Thank you for cheering my mood." Sameer said.

"Anytime, my love." Ishika smiled.

Talking along the way, they reached their destination. Sameer kissed her on the forehead and let her go before anyone notices them.

Sameer came to his room and jumped on his bed taking off his shoes. His day ended well, though in the morning he was irritated. He was lying on his bed smiling and reliving that kiss.

Suddenly, he remembered that he had to call Rohit to congratulate him.

Sameer picked up his phone and dialed Rohit.

"Hi! Sameer. How are you?" Rohit answered the call.

"Good. Actually, more than good."

"Hey! What's with the excitement?" Rohit asked confused.

"I have met someone. You will see at your wedding. And congratulations. I came to know your wedding date has been decided."

"Met who? Sameer, tell me. I can't wait till 14th Feb."

"Wait and you will know. And don't tell Siya and Jayesh."

"Okay. As you say."

"Okay. Let's meet at your wedding. Bye."

"Bye."

And the call ended.

CHAPTER NINE

Dates changed and Sameer and Ishika started getting to know each other more and more. They started spending most of their time together.

Sameer planned to take Ishika on a date, on the coming Sunday. Ishika, without hesitation agreed with him.

*

Ishika pulled on blue jeans and a peach-colored top with 'only for you' written on it with sequins. Sameer was flattened seeing her.

"You look...Ravishing." Sameer commented.

"Well, thank you." Ishika was pleased with his appraisal.

"Where was this beauty hidden for so many days?"

"It was waiting for the right moment to come out."

"Finally, that moment arrived."

"Yes. Only for you." Ishika said pointing at her top.

"Right. Only for me."

Sameer took her to one of the parks in the city. As it was Sunday, they found it a bit hard to find an auto-rickshaw that would take them to the park. All were busy carrying people. When the crowd got a little clear, they found one.

The vehicle drove them to their destination. It wasn't to their surprise that there was hustle-bustle of crowd everywhere outside the park. Street vendors shouted, calling people to buy their stuff. There was the honking of horns on the road due to traffic. Cheer from the crowd, traffic, and cries of vendors was all making the atmosphere chaotic.

Sameer and Ishika made their way to the park entrance. Sameer bought tickets for them and they headed in.

The walkway was covered with red cement tiles with patterns carved out on them. There were bushes and hedges about the height of the waist. Different flowering plants were planted. Some of them had newly budded flowers. They were brightly colored. As they walked, they saw small children playing on various rides in the park. They saw their cheerful faces. Their parents were screaming at them not to go out of their sight. At the center of the park was a huge lake where several other couples were seated. There were boats on the lake with people pedaling them through the way.

Sameer and Ishika also went boating. They carefully stepped onto the boat and took their seat. They pulled off from the edge, pedaling with their feet. Pedaling along the lake, they reached its far end where few birds were standing. There was no one to see them. They pulled closer to one of the birds but it flew away when the boat was a few inches from it. Ishika made a sad childish face at that. Sameer smiled at her expression and kissed her. He wouldn't miss a chance to romance. Ishika smiled shyly.

Sameer and Ishika pedaled to the side that had vividly colored flowers. Their smell could be recognized even from a distance. Sameer plucked one of them and tucked it in Ishika's hair.

"Boat No. 12, your time limit is over." A person at the boating edge announced.

Sameer and Ishika realized it was their boat. They rushed the boat, pedaling fast to reach the edge. They got off the boat and headed towards the ropeway counter.

There was a huge line. About twenty people were already waiting there. Sameer and Ishika got in the queue. On their turn, they entered a vessel that was more like a big basket with seats. The vessel began to ascend. Ishika wrapped Sameer in her arms. She was feeling afraid that she could fall. He unwrapped himself and put his hand around her waist.

“There is nothing to be afraid of.” He said convincingly.

Ishika looked around. The view of the park from above was panoramic. It was mesmerizing. The whole park was visible at that height. The whole lake can be captured in one glance. Lake water glistened in the sun. Ishika forgot her fear and started to love the ride and the view. The colorful flowers appeared like tiny spots on the ground. It wasn’t possible to distinguish between them. From that height, she could touch the leaves and twigs of tall trees. The cold breeze made the ride even more enjoyable. The atmosphere seemed so calm from above.

Ishika jumped in joy. She flew her hands in the air. The ride rode them around the whole park. The people appeared so tiny from above. On the way, her hands touched different trees. Several birds flew by near her. It was a wonderful and unforgettable experience for her.

The vessel finally came to a halt after taking a complete tour around the park. Ishika hugged Sameer after stepping out of the basket-like vessel. She thanked him for taking her on this ride.

It was evening and the sun was setting down. It was visible from the lake. Sameer and Ishika strolled towards an empty bench under a tree near the lake. Sameer sat on the bench holding her hand. Ishika rested her head on Sameer’s shoulder. And they watched the orange globe setting down, disappearing below the horizon. The reflection of the setting sun on the lake made it look like small flares on the water.

The sun was slowly hiding from the view. Birds were calling their kinds to return to their nests. Boats were coming to the edge, for closure of boating hours. Tall lights in the park turned on. The whole park glowed in the luminosity of lights. The cold breeze continued to blow and touch their faces. The atmosphere was serene and quiet. Suddenly, Ishika's phone rang. The screen displayed a number but no name. However, she instantly recognized it was her ex-boyfriend, Avinash. She didn't tell Sameer who it was. Instead, she slipped to a distance from where Sameer couldn't hear her and attended the call.

Sameer, unaware of the caller, waited there for Ishika to come back. She was talking on the phone for more than thirty minutes to an unsaved number. Sameer was growing impatient. He walked up to her asking who is on the other side. She muted the call and told him "It's Avinash. You go and sit there. I will be back in ten minutes."

Sameer returned to his place and kept waiting there, watching her talk. Her ten minutes lasted for another thirty minutes. Finally, she ended the call and came back to sit with Sameer.

"Who is Avinash?" Sameer asked.

His eyes were searching for answers.

"My ex-boyfriend," Ishika answered.

Sameer was awestruck. He felt that an arrow has pierced through his heart. His eyes were furious with rage. He clenched his fists in anger. But still, in his calm voice, he asked, "Why does he still have to call you?"

"He had some problem with his computer which he couldn't fix himself. He was just asking for my help." Ishika answered.

"Why does he have to call you when there are so many computer stores? And why didn't you tell me before that you have an ex-boyfriend?" He shouted at her.

Ishika trying to fight back her tears, putting her hand on Sameer's shoulder, said, "I don't know Sameer why he called me instead of going to any computer store. And I didn't tell you about him earlier because I didn't want to bring him up. That would have made you sad and myself even more. That relationship has been broken seven months ago and I have never spoken to him after our break-up until today. I love you, Sameer. Please forgive me."

Sameer didn't say a word. He was still furious. He grabbed her hand, stood up abruptly, and moved out of the park. Stopping the first cab he got, they stepped inside and headed to Sameer's hostel. On the way, Ishika kept pleading and apologizing. But Sameer didn't say a word or looked at her. Not even once. He was totally silent.

Along the way, he stopped by Ishika's room and asked her to step out of the car and go to her room. She refused. She didn't want to. She wanted to please Sameer. He asked her again. This time, in a high volume, probably scolding her. She did as she was asked. Ishika was going toward her room when Sameer stopped her, saying, "Ishika!"

She turned back in relief that he spoke.

"Yes?" She replied.

"Don't call or text me until I call you," Sameer warned, pulled up his taxi window, and gestured to the driver to leave.

Ishika got no time to react. With her head hung low in grief and guilt, she went to her room and lay on her mattress in whatever she was wearing. She didn't even bother to change. She was scolding herself, *why didn't she tell Sameer about her past relationship?*

Then another thought came to her mind, *if she had told him, it would have brought old memories and miseries to her again and to Sameer also. Maybe after knowing about it at first, he would have never accepted her.*

Emotional conflicts like this bombarded her mind. She wanted to call Sameer. She took out her phone. But then, she remembered his warning. She thought that if she calls, he will get even madder at her. So, she threw the phone away from her. She wanted to cry but her eyes were dry. She tried forcing the tears out of her eyes. But failed.

Sameer on the other hand reached his hostel and banged his door open. He shut the door furiously behind him. He hit his fist hard on the wall hurting his fingers in the process. He started to curse his relationship. His mind was blank after going through all this. At that moment, he could think of nothing but beating Avinash. In anger, he hit his fist again on the wall. Blood was visible now on his knuckles. There were bruises on the back of his fingers. He was moving around in his room absent-mindedly. Ishika's past had dawned on him. He was bare of thoughts. He started to clear his bed to distract himself. Under his pillow, he found a photograph of Ishika that he had clicked after sorting out their first fight. She looked damn beautiful in her profile view. Her shiny black hair, gleaming white teeth, pink lips, wide smile, and neckline made her photograph look even more gorgeous. Sameer paused for a minute and kept staring at the photograph. He used to keep this photograph under his pillow every night. It made him feel like she is sleeping beside him.

After staring at the photograph for a while, Sameer lifted it in his hands and tore it in half. Ishika's smile and below were in one half and upper features in the other half. He tore it to even more tiny bits and flew them in the air outside the window. A gust of wind touched his face. He quickly closed the window and moved to his bed changing into his nightwear. He lay on his bed. Both hands under his head, his eyes fixed on the ceiling, he was trying to sink in everything Ishika was trying to explain.

Sameer didn't sleep all night in frustration. It was too hard for him to forget whatever had happened. The only thought running through his mind was that Ishika betrayed him. She kept him in the dark all this while. She cheated on him. She should have told him earlier. Though he would be sad or angry with her for a moment, he would have eventually understood. If she had told him before, things wouldn't have gone this ugly. For the whole night, he was thinking about all this.

CHAPTER TEN

The sun came up welcoming a brand new day. But Sameer was still stuck with what had happened yesterday. He was deprived of sleep. His eyes were red and sore. His face looked dull and weary. He looked at the clock. There was still an hour left for his class. But being fed up staying in the room along with his gloom, he took his bag, hung it on his shoulder, and left without breakfast for his class.

Sameer entered the college gate and spotted Ishika from a distance. She was waiting in the playground, probably for him. From that distance, he could tell that she was sad. But he didn't care. Hiding from her eyes, he walked towards his classroom. But she saw him anyway and called to him. He ignored her call and continued walking. So, she came running to him. He still wasn't looking at her. She tried making up for yesterday, but he stopped her mid-sentence and left.

In the class, he struggled to focus on what the professor was teaching. He couldn't. He sat for about fifteen minutes there, trying to take in everything that was being taught. But his mind was elsewhere. Uninterested, he left the classroom without giving any reason to the professor. The whole class along with the professor was stunned at his angry face. Everyone kept staring at him as he made his way out of the class. He didn't bother to look back.

Coming out of the academic building, he saw Ishika sitting alone in the playground and crying in the blazing heat of the sun. she was all wet in sweat. But she didn't seem to care. She was only crying. Sameer couldn't see her in tears. He went to her and put his hand on her shoulder from behind. She lifted her head to see who it was. Sameer's anger vanished in seconds after seeing her moist eyes. He sat down in front of her and held her head close to his chest. Wiping her tears, he stopped her crying. He hugged her and said, "Sorry, I was mad at you since yesterday", apologizingly. She wrapped her hands around him and held her head to his chest.

"I am really sorry Sameer that I hurt you by not telling you about my past relationship at first." She said, still in a heavy voice.

"No dear. I hurt you by being angry at you for no reason. I should have listened to your explanation." Sameer said in a soothing voice.

"From now on, if we are angry with each other, we will not talk for a day and everything will be back to normal on the next day. Agree?" She demanded.

"Agreed." He said.

They sat in the sun hugged, in one another's arms until the college bell rang. When the bell rang, a crowd of students emerged and Sameer and Ishika left from the college gate skipping the rest of their classes.

Ishika took Sameer to her room. He moved his eyes all around her room. His eyes fell on her maroon underwear hanging near the window. Ishika noticed his gaze and quickly took and hid it under the mattress feeling embarrassed. Her room had a mattress on the floor, a study table, and a cupboard. Pretty much, it was like any regular student's room.

Sameer was standing near the mattress. He held Ishika's hand and pulled her towards himself. They fell on the mattress, Ishika on Sameer.

"Ouch", Sameer cried in pain.

Ishika giggled.

Ishika moved to the side getting down from Sameer's body. Sameer's eyes were fixed on Ishika's face. She was so beautiful. Her shiny white eyes, stooping nose, short pink lips–everything added to her beauty. With his fingers, he tucked her hair from her face to behind her ears.

Sameer moved his eyes to check if the door was locked and fixed them back on Ishika. His hand moved to her waist. They could feel the intimacy of the moment in their hearts. His fingers crawled inside her top all the way up to her breasts. He touched them and squeezed them. Ishika sighed in pain. Both of them were feeling a rush of adrenaline, they had never felt before. He pulled off her top and removed his t-shirt.

Taking his hand on Ishika's back Sameer pulled her closer. Her breasts touched his chest. They didn't know whether it was right or wrong. They just knew it was real. Ishika pulled her jeans off and unbuttoned Sameer's. They were lying naked. The euphoria of love and adrenaline rush added to their intimate desire. The next moment, he was upon her. He kissed her on the side of her neck. His lips moved to her face. He kissed her eyes, and nose and came to touch her lips. Both of them kissed each other. They could feel each other's moist lips. At times, their tongues touched. The moistness of their lips didn't want them to stop. His lips came down from her face. He sucked her nipples. Bit them. Ishika groaned. Lifting his face, looking into Ishika's eyes, Sameer entered inside her. She screamed silently in pain and pleasure simultaneously, wanting more. He pulled in, harder. She screamed more. And for the next minutes, they had sex.

Finished and satisfied, Sameer asked, "Was it good?"

"It was awesome." She replied smiling.

They kept lying there without clothes for the next few hours cuddling in one another's arms, feeling each other to the best they could.

CHAPTER ELEVEN

Rohit's marriage was nearing. Back in Udaipur, he was busy with wedding purchases of clothes, jewelry, gifts, decoration accessories, etc. He and Jayesh were busy all day distributing wedding cards, making arrangements for the comfortable stay of guests, plan for the wedding rituals, deciding what cuisines will be made, and other wedding requirements.

Siya was occupied with her own wedding arrangements like what to wear for seven circles around the sacred fire; what to wear for other rituals and reception; what different kinds of jewelry she should try; which one will look best on her; how will she look in front of Rohit in her bridal attire; what will he think of her get up. Overall, she was truly satisfied that she is marrying the boy she loves. She was happy that Rohit's father had rejected dowry at once. Even after being insisted many times by her parents, Rohit's father was tough at his decision. His words were, "You are giving your beloved daughter to us. That's a whole lot to accept. I can't take or demand anything more from you. We will never be able to repay you for happily giving your daughter. I am truly thankful to you for this from my heart."

These words won everyone's heart in Siya's family. Her cousins were busy discussing their dresses; who will steal Rohit's shoes and how much to demand in return for his shoes. Siya always warned them that they should not demand anything, but cousins are cousins. They never listen. They often teased Siya about her first night with Rohit. They asked, "What would you do, Siya? Tell us. Don't be shy."

Hiding her smile between her lips, Siya would reply, "I will not do anything. He will do whatever he wants and I will just help him in that?"

To that, her cousins shouted, "Aww...", in unison, making Siya feel shy.

Sameer arrived with Ishika to Udaipur on the 13th of February, being Rohit's and Siya's marriage on the 14th. At first, Ishika wasn't willing to come with him. But on Sameer's sweet insist, she agreed to attend the wedding. Coming out of the station, Sameer called a cab. They got in and Sameer dropped Ishika at her house, planting a kiss on her lips before leaving for his home.

Sameer's mother welcomed him by spreading her arms in front of her. Sameer gave her a brief hug and touched his father's feet. Being tired, he ate dinner and went to sleep.

Ishika's parents were surprised to see her return home without a holiday. They didn't know she was coming. She informed them that she has come to attend her friend's wedding ceremony. Anyway, they were happy to see their daughter. She was also tired, so she too ate and slept without talking to Sameer that night.

It was 14th February. Valentine's Day and Rohit and Siya's wedding day. A memorable one for them.

Sameer woke up early. He got ready, had breakfast in time, and went out to market. He had to buy two gifts today.

One for Rohit and Siya as their wedding gift. Second for Ishika as her Valentine's Day gift.

First, Sameer went inside a gift shop. It had a huge display of sculptures and models made of mud or cement. They all were too attractive to not buy. The shopkeeper showed him a range of models according to his demand and description. Sameer had a hard time choosing one of them. It took him about half an hour to decide on one. It had a tree near a pond surrounded by hills behind the back. Under the tree, sat a boy and girl holding a heart together in their hands. He requested the shopkeeper to wrap it as a gift, paid him, took the model, and left.

Then, Sameer went inside a jewelry shop. He requested the jeweler to show him necklaces for a girl around the age of twenty. The jeweler showed him a wide range of necklaces, from gold and silver to diamond and pearl. They all were shining in the bright light inside the shop. Sameer was once again in the dilemma of choice. Again, he couldn't decide which one would look best on Ishika. He told the jeweler to show some with the alphabet 'I'. The jeweler did as he was told. Eventually, he decided to buy the one that had 'I' at the center with gold and silver stones and pellets around it. This one too, he wrapped as a gift, paid, and returned home.

In the evening, Sameer called Ishika to get dressed in an hour. They have to reach the wedding venue. He would be waiting outside her house. Ishika hurried around to find the perfect dress for her in the closet. She took out a Rosso Corsa lehenga and blouse, worked and laced with gold-colored sequins and stones. She got herself ready with the dress-up and make-up and ran out saying to her mother, "bye".

Sameer was waiting outside as he had told. He was wearing a dark turquoise suit and a white shirt. they both complemented each other and Ishika sat on Sameer's bike holding him by his waist. He raced his bike to the wedding venue.

Sameer parked his bike near the venue and went inside with Ishika, holding her by her waist. Ishika removed his hand. He kept his hand again on her waist, so she let him and went inside.

The venue was a huge garden meant for occasions. At the venue entrance, two pillars were stalled. They were decorated with colorful artificial flowers, leaves, and vines. A red carpet was laid out from the entrance straight to the wedding stage, curving around the fountain in the middle. The fountain was quite big with multi-colored lights changing frequently from one color to another. Soft music also played in a low sound at the fountain. There was a music band on one side consisting of two male and two female singers. They were singing 90's Bollywood melodies. On the other side, was an array of food stalls having starters, desserts, mains, and sides with a server at each food item. Several tables and chairs were set in the whole garden. Some were occupied by the guests, while some guests were moving around with nothing to do.

Rohit and Jayesh were speaking to each other near the wedding stage when they saw Sameer, coming with a girl. Jayesh was expressionless seeing him with a girl with his hand around her waist. Rohit was smiling, looking at Jayesh's face. On the inside, he too was surprised. Then he suddenly remembered Sameer had told him that he has met someone. He understood, that someone is his girlfriend and she is here. Rohit waved his hand to Sameer to call him. Sameer and Ishika went towards them. Sameer introduced Rohit and Jaysh to Ishika and Ishika to them.

"Meet his girlfriend", Rohit said to Jayesh chuckling.

Jayesh passed him a disgusted look.

"Where is the bride?" Sameer asked.

"In her room, getting ready for me," Rohit answered pointing towards a two-storied building.

"By the way, I have to get dressed properly. You guys have a seat and chat." Rohit said and left towards the building he was previously pointing to.

Sameer, Ishika, and Jayesh sat, occupying one of the tables, and were talking.

There was an announcement from the music band.

"Ladies and gentlemen, brace yourself for the moment we all have been waiting for on this auspicious day."

Everyone's attention turned to the band.

"Please welcome our handsome groom with a thundering round of applause", said another announcement as Rohit was coming out of the building in his well-groomed clothes. He was wearing a shiny dark brown suit with a cream-colored shirt and red tie printed with tiny patterns.

The wedding stage was all set with the sacred fire flaming and a priest sitting by it and waiting for the bride-groom.

Rohit walked to the stage and sat near the fire opposite the priest.

The next announcement said, "Here comes our beautiful bride."

Guests clapped and cheered again.

Siya was wearing a red saree and a lot of jewelry. Her saree was heavily worked with stones and laces and she looked beautiful in it.

She walked up to the stage and sat beside Rohit.

"Happy Valentine's Day, my love", she whispered in Rohit's ears.

"Happy Valentine's Day to you too, sweetheart", he replied.

"Where is my Valentine's Day gift?" She demanded.

"Right beside you", Rohit whispered and smiled.

She too chuckled shyly.

The priest started with the mantras. At times, he told Rohit and Siya to throw something kept on a plate in front of them in the sacred fire. For most of the time, Rohit and Siya were glancing at each other from the corner of their eyes. They could sense each other's happiness in one another's eyes. While reciting one of the mantras, the priest told Rohit to put vermillion *(sindoor)* on Siya's scalp. While reading another, he said Rohit to tie *mangalsutra* around her neck. At last, they stood up for moving seven rounds around the sacred fire. "These seven rounds are meant for seven promises that the husband and wife are expected to abide by their whole life." The priest said.

Everyone was showering them with flowers and petals, while they were moving around the fire. They completed the seven circles and with that, the priest declared them married.

Rohit and Siya touched everyone's feet—priest, Rohit's parents, and Siya's parents to take their blessings. Rohit kissed Siya on her forehead and they went to their respective room.

The wedding stage was now converted into a one for reception. Two royal throne chairs were kept there, removing the sacred pit *(hawan-kund)*. Meanwhile, guests had gathered at the food stalls to try out different food items. The band was singing as usual.

After an hour, Rohit and Siya emerged again from inside the building, this time together. They walked up to the stage, holding hands, accompanied by their parents and relatives. Rohit and Siya took their seat on the royal throne chairs and their parents and relatives stood by their sides.

After a while, guests walked up to the stage to congratulate the newly wedded couple and give them gifts. Rohit and Siya thanked them in response. One by one, many guests congratulated them and gave their blessings. Sameer, Ishika, and Jayesh also went up the stage when most of the guests were done and had left. Siya was surprised to see Ishika. Rohit informed her that she is with Sameer.

"She is Ishika. The girl who is lucky to have me, just like you said. Remember, Siya?" Sameer said to Siya introducing Ishika to her.

"Why didn't you tell me before, Sameer?" Siya asked.

"I wanted it to be a surprise," Sameer replied.

"Thank you, Ishika for being with my lonely hopeless friend. Please do not ever leave him." Siya pleased Ishika.

"Never Siya di." Ishika promised.

"Di? Just call me Siya."

"Ok, Siya. And congratulations to both of you."

Rohit and Siya thanked her together. Sameer handed them the present and they cleared the stage for other guests.

Sameer, Ishika, and Jayesh had the most delicious dinner ever. After that, they left.

Sameer stopped somewhere between the wedding venue and Ishika's house, finding the road empty and quiet. Only the street lights showed their presence. He kissed Ishika and knelt before her. From the pocket of his pant, he took out the gift and holding it with his hands gave it to her, wishing her, "Happy Valentine's Day".

Ishika took the gift from Sameer's hand excitedly. She unwrapped it. The surface of the box felt like velvet. She opened the box and gasped. She found a necklace inside. She took it out hanging it in her fingers. She told Sameer to tie it around her neck. She looked even prettier in her lehenga with the necklace. Ishika hugged him and they were again on the bike.

Sameer stopped by Ishika's house. They got off the bike and Ishika was heading towards the door of her house. But after a few steps, she came running back and kissed Sameer. They kissed for another minute. Neighbors could watch them anytime from anywhere, so they didn't wait for long there and with that kiss, they ended their first Valentine's Day together. They said to each other good-bye and left for their own houses.

CHAPTER TWELVE

The next morning, at around 10 a.m., Sameer called Rohit and Jayesh to meet. They were too tired from the wedding arrangements and needed rest. But Sameer told them that he would bring Ishika with him and they have to leave tomorrow for Dehradun. At the mention of Ishika's name, Rohit and Jayesh got charged up. They definitely wanted to meet the girl who has cast her magic on a boy like Sameer. Siya was listening to their conversation quietly, lying beside Rohit. She instantly jumped up between their conversation and said, "Ok, Sameer. Done. We will meet at our usual spot at 6 p.m."

Sameer was excited that Ishika will get to meet his friends properly.

Sameer then called Ishika and informed her about their get-together. She hesitantly agreed.

In the evening, at the decided time, they all reached Fateh Sagar Lake. Ishika came with Sameer, Siya with Rohit and Jayesh came alone.

Sameer's friend wanted to meet Ishika. They were excited and happy to see her. They shot a thousand questions at her, like, when did you two start to notice each other; how did she convince Sameer; what was Sameer's reaction; for how long they are together.

Ishika was taken aback by their questions in one go. She started to feel embarrassed. Siya noticed her embarrassment. She went to her and supported Ishika by her shoulder.

"No need to answer them, Ishika." Siya persuaded her.

"No, no. It is okay. I have no problem answering them. This is the first time I am getting faced with such questions. So, I felt a little uncomfortable." Ishika said.

"In case, you want," Siya said.

Then, one by one, Ishika answered all of Rohit's and Jayesh's questions. Sameer sat back looking at everyone's faces as she answered. He was happy to see that she liked their company.

Ishika kept talking to them for more than an hour. Siya could see how happy Sameer was. She wished that they always stay together, just like she stayed with Rohit. Rohit and Jayesh shared some of the stupid things Sameer did with them. Sameer gestured them not to. But friends don't listen.

While they were talking, Ishika's phone beeped. There was a message from her mother saying her to get home in time. She messaged her back that she will be back there in thirty minutes. She had to leave the wonderful conversation unfinished. She stood up to leave. Sameer told her to wait, he will drop her home. They all stood up, shook hands, hugged, and then everyone was on their way back home.

The next day, Sameer and Ishika met at the station to return to Dehradun.

The train arrived and they boarded it. The train ran along the tracks taking them to Dehradun.

CHAPTER THIRTEEN

Sameer was in the final semester of his curriculum. He had to invest more time in his studies than usual. He started to give Ishika a little less time. Now, he didn't sit with her at the college playground between lecture breaks. In college, he met her only during lunch break. Then, he would talk to her only at night. Most of his time was devoted to books.

Ishika was feeling quite low due to this. But she also understood that Sameer was right. She knew, that if Sameer don't study well, he wouldn't be able to achieve his dream. So, she didn't say anything. She accepted the fact that for the time being, studies are Sameer's priority.

Days went by and Sameer's exam came nearer. He stayed awake till midnight to complete his lessons. In his class, he listened more attentively and tried to take note of all the important things. He barely got time now during the day to talk to Ishika. He could talk to her only after midnight. Ishika was dying to talk to him like before. But she had no chance until Sameer's exams are over.

Finally, Sameer's exams started. He slept and woke up surrounded by his books. He was serious with his exams. He had to do well to get a proper job, so that, he could save some money for his dream. One by one, he wrote his exams with his best knowledge.

And exams eventually ended. This was a relief for him and more relief for Ishika. Now they could talk for hours and there is nothing to disturb them. Ishika was happier than Sameer for this.

Before a day when Sameer had to go back home and leave his hostel, he took Ishika a day out. He took her for lunch at a restaurant. He ordered Ishika's favorite food and watched her smile as she ate. Getting out of the restaurant, he took her to an Aurelia store. He bought her a bright yellow-orange kurti. Even after Ishika's insist that he shouldn't buy, she already had many, he didn't listen. It was his last day in Dehradun and Sameer wanted to make it special. He wanted it to be one of the happiest days of her life.

After lunch and shopping, Ishika took Sameer to her room. She opened the door and locked it behind her. She jumped on Sameer. He held her up in his arms and she kissed her. He kissed back. And the kiss continued for another five minutes. Removing her lips, Ishika said, "Thank you, Sameer for everything you did today. It made my day."

"I love you, Ishika darling." He said and they fell on the mattress.

Their intimate desires came alive and they undressed each other. Sameer was lying on Ishika, kissing her from forehead to her naval, kissing her eyes, nose, lips, neck, breasts, and curve on the way down. He was inside her, the next minute. They had sex. Ishika smiled with pain. She was satisfied at the highest. Sameer kissed her forehead and pulled her towards him getting touched by her breasts. Cuddled into each other, staring into each other's eyes, they slept.

CHAPTER FOURTEEN

Sameer was back at his home, while Ishika had still a year left for her studies to complete. After almost two years of living together, they were now in a long-distance relationship. As Sameer was now free most of the time, they talked almost whole day on the phone. Whenever they wanted to see each other, they did it on video calls. Meeting in person was not possible now. No matter, how long they saw and talked to each other on video calls, they were never satisfied. They still craved spending time together. They missed each other. They missed their dates, their hugs, their kisses, and many other things. More than everything, they missed being together.

After a month, Sameer's result was declared. He ranked among the Top 10 students in his college. His constant determination, devotion, and hard work during the last days of his preparation had paid off well. His parents were proud of his performance. They gifted a sweet box full of laddoos to their relatives and neighbors.

With results, came another responsibility to Sameer. He needed a job now to support his family. He started looking for a job of his choice. He applied to a few companies and organizations that were into scientific research. He was called for an interview by some of them. But he didn't meet the expected requirements of some of them, while others didn't offer him a good salary. With quite a struggle, he passed the interview of 'BIO-RESEARCH INDIA'. The organization agreed to offer him a starting salary of Rs. 25,000 per month and an annual bonus. The organization was based in Delhi. It was oriented toward research on different biological species and preparing a data analysis on their use and harmful effects on humans. This data was further used for the improvement and modification of the species in favor of humans. Sameer's job was confirmed. He signed all the documents required and waited for his date of joining.

While talking to Ishika, Sameer informed her about his job confirmation. She was delighted to know. She wanted to come to Udaipur for a day to celebrate the news with him. But Sameer stopped her and persuaded her to not come before her holidays. She agreed.

Sameer also gave this news to Rohit, Siya, and Jayesh. They were excited and demanded a night-out party from him. Sameer couldn't refuse. He agreed for the Saturday night. They shouted 'congratulations', in chorus.

After a few days of Sameer's interview and job confirmation, his joining date was confirmed. He had to move to Delhi. His job was to do basic research on the given sample and register the data. He loved his job but he wasn't satisfied. He wanted to become a full-time artist and open his own Art & Craft Institute, where he could teach budding artists and make them aware of the scope of art in this world.

Days passed. He went to work as usual in the morning and returned home in the evening. He used to make his food himself. Again, he couldn't give all of his daytime to Ishika. He called her for a short while during lunch hours and was able to talk to her properly only at night.

Now the hard phase of their life had begun. Sameer was occupied with his work all day. And Ishika waited for the nightfall every day, so that, she could talk to Sameer.

Sameer began saving a part of his salary as an investment for his institute. After about ten months of doing his job, he had enough savings to open the institute on a small scale.

Sameer started planning on how to open the institute; how he would run it; how much time should he invest in that; how to manage his job and institute at the same time. He didn't want to resign from his job at once, as soon as he opens the institute.

Sameer had to work hard. In the morning, he had to go to his job and in the evening, he was busy for his institute. He bought a space that was on sale for a shop, prepared all the required documents, and signed them. He needed permission from various authorities which he had to approach several times. Often, his appointment with the officials was rejected. But he kept running to their offices, almost every day. At one point, he started to lose hope. He thought it isn't in his reach to own the institute. He is only made to work for others.

During his hard times, when Sameer was struggling for his dream, Ishika was there for him. She stood by his side and gave him strength and hope, that he will eventually pass through this hard time and achieve his dream.

Ishika's words filled Sameer with a new hope. Approaching the officials regularly finally paid off. He eventually got the required permissions and was all set to convert the space he bought into an Art & Craft Institute.

The space had an entrance at the front that became the back of his institute. Opposite the entrance, was his demonstration table. In front of his demonstration table, were set several benches and desks for students to sit and work. The walls of the institute were colored brightly. Different paintings and murals decorated the colorful walls. The board outside the institute read–'THE ART WORLD – An Art & Craft Institute'.

Ishika, Sameer's friends, and his parents were delighted to know about the opening of his own institute. They wished him good luck.

On the Grand Opening day of his institute, Sameer invited a famous artist, local to Delhi as the Chief Guest. Together, they gave a free demo class to a group of about thirty students. Students praised them. They liked their way of demonstrating and teaching. Each step and the process were quite simple and sophisticated.

In a span of 2-3 months, Sameer's institute started to do well. He had a group of seventy students, divided into batches according to their age groups. From children of age 5 years to youngsters of age 25 years came to his institute to learn various forms and styles of art. They also learned to upcycle old and waste materials to make something creative. Something 'out of the box'.

Sameer now decided to resign from his job and focus only on his institute. He devoted his whole time for teaching and demonstrating his creative skills to his students. Students acquired new innovative ideas to improve their art skills. Sameer used to earn about Rs.

35,000 per month from his institute which was more than what he earned at BIO-RESEARCH INDIA, where he worked once. He was satisfied and happy.

CHAPTER FIFTEEN

There was a business summit in Delhi where various entrepreneurs, who have recently started their own businesses were invited. Sameer was also invited. The entrepreneurs shared their visions and ideas with the audience. The organizers presented Sameer, with an award for 'BEST GROWING BUSINESS'. His level of excitement was nowhere on the ground. He had achieved what he had never expected or dreamed.

There, at the summit, Sameer met Rishi Sahdev, a rising phenomenon in the world of singing. He congratulated Sameer on his achievement. He too was a fan of art, although he was not an artist. Sameer told him about Ishika. He showed Rishi a video on his phone in which she was singing at the college fest. Rishi loved her voice.

"We need such talented singers in the industry." He said.

"I would like to meet her personally. Here is my office address. Come there anytime with her." He handed Sameer his visiting card and left.

Sameer looked forward to seeing Ishika as an established singer. He called Ishika as soon as he reached his apartment.

"Hi, Ishika. I have two good news for you today." Sameer couldn't control his excitement.

"Take a breath, Sameer. What's the news?"

"One, I received an award for 'BEST GROWING BUSINESS' and second, I met Rishi Sahdev today at the summit. He wants to meet you in person."

"What! Aren't you joking?" Ishika couldn't believe what she heard just now.

"Do I seem to joke?" Sameer asked.

"Seriously? A singer like Rishi Sahdev wants to meet me? Thank you, Sameer. I can't tell you how happy I am."

"Come to Delhi as soon as you can."

"I will come right now if you say."

"Stop kidding. Board the next train and come here soon."

"As you say, sir. Bye."

"Bye."

Ishika boarded the train from Dehradun to Delhi the next day. Her joy and enthusiasm had no limit.

Ishika reached Delhi, stepped out of the train, and hugged Sameer as soon as she saw him. She thanked him several times. Sameer took her to his institute first. She gasped at the beauty of the institute walls. She had never seen such amazing paintings and murals. She kept staring at them and was lost in them. Sameer's jolt brought her back. He then took her to his apartment and let her rest for the day.

The next day, Sameer fixed an appointment with Rishi. He took Ishika to his office. A lady at the reception told them to wait while Rishi is in a meeting. They had to wait for more than an hour. Finally, Rishi came out of the meeting hall and called Sameer and Ishika inside his cabin.

Rishi's cabin was filled with music albums, CDs, awards, and certificates. Ishika started to get nervous in front of him. She still couldn't believe that she was called by him.

"Hi, Ishika. Welcome to my office. How are you doing?" Rishi asked her.

"Aa...Aa...I am doing fine, sir. Thank you for inviting me here." She stammered due to nervousness.

"You don't need to be nervous."

"Sorry, sir."

"Don't say sorry to me. Instead thank Sameer, who showed me your wonderful talent."

"Right sir."

"So, would you like to sing a cover song that I was offered to sing?" He offered.

"Of course, sir. I would love it."

Rishi along with Sameer and Ishika went to the recording studio. He handed the lyrics to Ishika and asked her to sing. To her astonishment, she sang exceptionally well even though she was nervous. Rishi, Sameer, and others praised her with applause. Sameer kissed her and said, "Good job, sweetheart."

Rishi informed Ishika that the song will be released in a week. It will be live on television and social media.

"Congratulations to you on your first song." He appreciated.

After a week, the song was released. Ishika made her public debut appearance at the song launch in Delhi. She was overjoyed and excited to see the public cheer for her, say out her name, shutterbugs clicking her pictures, all the fame. At the launch, she sang a part of the song and the crowd cheered.

Sameer was watching her from a distance. He was happy for her. He wanted to help her become a singer and he did it.

Ishika's song was a grand success. It crossed over 100 million views within a week of release. It became trending on social media. Television channels increased its popularity even more. She was on cloud nine at her success.

After a few months, Ishika was approached for another song by a music producer. She was called to Mumbai and she was offered to sing the song for them. She didn't refuse the offer. It was what she had always wanted. To become a singer and be the best of them all.

Ishika's second song was also a success. In fact, more than the first one. It crossed over 150 million views on social media in 2-3 days of release. She had become the new sensational star.

She had earned enough money from her last two songs that she can now live on her own. She could now bear her own expenses. So, she left her studies incomplete and moved to Mumbai. She bought an apartment of her own there.

Ishika's parents saw her on television one day. Flipping through the channels, they saw her giving an interview to the media about her journey as a singer. She shared her personal life, her educational life, and how she got to meet Rishi and he offered her her first song. Her parents were dazed. Her mother was angry at her that she left her studies and she didn't inform her parents before doing all this. But she was more happy than angry for her. Her daughter had become a superstar and now she is on TV. Her father, on the other hand, was mad at her that she became a singer. He hated singers, remember? Her mother watched her full interview, while her father stood up and went to his room. He couldn't bear the sight of her, anymore.

After the interview was finished, Ishika's mother called her.

"Hi, mom," Ishika said.

"How are you, *beta*?" Her mother asked.

"I am fine, mom. How are you?"

"I am also fine, *beta*. Congratulations on your success."

"Thank you, mom."

"Wait a minute, your father wants to speak to you." Her mother said.

"Your daughter is on the line. Talk to her." Her mother said to her father.

"I don't want to talk to her. She is dead to me." Her father refused angrily.

"Talk to her at least once." Her mother insisted.

"Leave me alone, I said." Her father said sternly to her mother.

"Don't mind his words, *beta*. You know his hate for singers." Ishika's mother said to her going away from her father.

"I know, mom. You don't worry." She said.

"When are you coming home?" Her mother asked.

"I am not coming home until my father calls me. I am living a happy life, here in Mumbai."

"Oh, come on, *beta*. You know that's never going to happen. Come once at least to see your mother."

"No, mom. You can come to me if you want."

"I can't come, you know very well."

"Then wait for an uncertain period to meet your daughter. Anyway, I will talk to you later, mom. Bye."

"Bye, *beta*."

CHAPTER SIXTEEN

Ishika and Sameer were well settled and followed their dream. They were doing exceptionally well in their fields.

Sameer now collaborated with various artists, made art installations for various brands and organizations, and managed his institute.

Ishika, on the other hand, was getting more and more song offers. She also started to get advertisement offers from different brands. The brands and singing paid her well. She became rich. In fact, she earned more than Sameer. Somewhere, deep inside, she felt proud of this. She was happy with her career. It was all she wanted since her childhood and she didn't want to go back to her family.

Life, work, relationship, and personal time were in sync with each other for both Sameer and Ishika.

Now, both of them couldn't give each other most of their time. They were occupied with work all day. They got too tired due to work. Only 1-2 hours of conversation at night was enough for them. Sometimes, even that was impossible if one of them slept early.

Sameer was often invited to various inaugurals and events to make eye-catching art installations. He was also appointed as a judge for some Art & Craft competitions. He often conducted 1-day or 2-days workshops. He too organized competitions exclusively for his students at his institute. He also did collaborations with other artists. Several new brands approached him to design an attractive logo for them and had to meet their deadlines. He too somewhat became a public figure.

Ishika was busy singing new songs for producers. She now had to go to various award events. She used to organize concerts in various cities across India. She was also invited as a guest in reality shows. Various brands now started approaching her to advertise their products and services. She was also nominated and won awards for her sweet and melodious voice.

These things made their schedules very busy and hectic. It was hard for them to find some time for themselves and for each other.

For many days, Sameer had been thinking of proposing to Ishika for marriage. But he was low on confidence. He didn't know how he should propose – should he ask her directly or give her clues to solve? What if she says, "Not now, Sameer"? What if she asks for time to decide? Hows' and what ifs' filled his mind with questions and doubts.

With much thinking and scratching his mind for several days, Sameer finally decided to ask her directly by taking her out on a date.

Sameer asked Ishika to get a day off, he is coming to Mumbai to meet her. Searching through her busy schedule, she decided on a date. She was delighted that she will finally get to meet him after so many months of waiting.

Sameer arrived at the station. Ishika was already waiting there for him. Sameer stepped off the train coach and moved his head towards her to kiss her. But she stopped him, saying, “Not here.”

They walked out of the station. The time was 1 p.m. and it was extremely hot. They decided to go to a movie, so that, they will escape the heat for now and by the time movie will end, it would be evening.

They reached the movie theatre and booked the corner seats at the back. People were settling down in their seats. The theatre lights dimmed and the movie started. Sameer was still thinking about his proposal. In the darkness, his hand moved on Ishika’s breast. He grabbed and squeezed it. But she removed his hand. He put his hand again. She removed it again. He couldn’t understand why was she acting so unromantic and weird today. He watched the movie occupied by his thoughts. The movie ended at 4:35 p.m. and they came out of the theatre.

Ishika took Sameer to one of the famous parks. The park was beautiful. Many statues and sculptures were installed at various places. There were fountains and small waterfalls. An orchestra band was singing romantic songs. Children were playing with their parents. Couples were busy with each other. Sameer was stunned at the beauty of the park.

After spending some time in the park, Ishika took Sameer to one of the most expensive restaurants in Mumbai. The waiter handed them a menu card. There were so many dishes to confuse him about which one to choose. Sameer offered Ishika to order. Among the Indian, Chinese, Italian, and Continental, she chose Italian. She ordered *spaghetti alle vongole*, a noodle dish and *tiramisu*, an Italian dessert. The dishes were quite expensive.

The food was served. Sameer liked the food very much. Leaving his food in the middle of eating, he stood up and returned with his washed hands. He knelt in front of Ishika holding a small red velvet box in his hand. He opened it in front of her. There was a diamond ring inside. Ishika was surprised. *What is he doing,* she thought.

"I want to marry you. Will you become my better half for the rest of my life?" Sameer finally proposed.

Ishika was dazed. She couldn't tell anything for a minute.

"I can't marry you, Sameer." She spoke.

"But, why?" He asked surprised by her refusal.

"I don't feel the same for you now."

"What happened? You once wanted to marry me and now you are refusing."

"I told you, I don't feel the same for you."

"Why?"

"Are you sure that you want to know?"

"Yes."

"You are not my type, not anymore. I want someone who takes me out every weekend. Someone, who takes me out for dinner at least twice a month. Someone, who always surprises me with expensive gifts. Someone, who is willing to leave his parents to live with me. Someone, who earns more than me, or at least, around it. You will not be able to fulfill my expectations and demands, Sameer. Moreover, I earn a lot more than you do. If it was on you, you would have never brought me to such an expensive place. I deserve someone better than you, Sameer. You are just an insignificant artist and nothing more."

Sameer, putting the ring back in his pocket, stood up and sat back on the chair.

"Why didn't you tell me all this before?" He asked.

"Because I thought you are too busy to listen." She answered.

"Now what?"

"It's over between us. Thank you for everything you did for me. And don't get disheartened. You will get someone who deserves you. Be angry with me. I have no problem. But please, leave me alone from now on."

"What about the promise you made to Siya?"

"That promise no more matters."

Sameer stood up thrusting his chair back. He asked the waiter for the bill. The bill was, Rs. 4,330. He took out the money from his pocket, kept it on the table in front of Ishika, and left.

Ishika just sat there like she didn't care. She had become a superstar. Success and fame took over her mind. She forgot to step on the ground as she continued to grow with fame and money. She was flying high in the air with clouds of money all around her. She forgot, how she proposed to Sameer; how she was yelling at him when he got angry; the promise she made to Siya; everything. It was Sameer who helped her become a singer. But she didn't care now about all that. She was high.

Ishika's insensible rejection broke Sameer. He immediately left for Delhi on the next flight. On the way, he deleted her phone number and every picture of her. He threw the diamond ring in the sea on his way to the airport. He tried fighting back his tears along the whole way.

Sameer was back in Delhi in his apartment. He cried for hours after he reached. He wanted to delete every memory of her from his mind. All their moments together came flashing back in his mind, which made him cry even more.

For once in his life, he had encouraged himself to get into a relationship, and that relationship, those feelings, all changed when Ishika got fame and money. He screamed in the pain of heartbreak. Tears kept rolling down his eyes. He kept crying until his eyes ran out of tears.

CHAPTER SEVENTEEN

Sameer was very much disturbed for the next few days. He was still trying to handle his agony. He still looked miserable and weary. His eyes looked swollen and had dark circles around them due to lack of sleep.

One morning, he called his parents and told them, he wants to marry. His parents sensed something was wrong from his heavy and stammering voice.

"What happened, son?" They asked.

"Nothing," he answered.

"You seem sad. Your voice is heavy. Were you crying?" His mother asked.

"No, mom. I just want to marry and settle down. That's all."

"But why all of a sudden?"

"It just came to my mind last night," he reasoned.

His parents could sense something was wrong, however, they didn't force him to speak.

"Ok, son. We will start looking for a girl for you," his parents agreed.

"One more thing."

"Yes?"

"She should be a small-town girl."

"Why, *beta*? What's the matter?"

"Nothing. It is my choice."

And he ended the call.

His parents did as they were asked. They started looking for a girl for Sameer, keeping in mind that she should be a small-town girl. They told all their relatives to look for the best girl for Sameer.

After taking the shower, Sameer called Siya. She didn't answer. He tried two more times. But the call remained unanswered. In despair, he kept his phone away from him and started making breakfast for himself.

Sameer came out of the kitchen with his breakfast. His phone rang. He kept his plate on the dining table and picked up the call. It was Siya.

"Sorry, Sameer. I couldn't answer when you called. I was sleeping," she apologized.

"It's ok, Siya," he said.

"Why did you call, by the way?"

"Is Rohit around?"

"No."

"I called to ask you something about myself?"

"What is it?"

"How unworthy am I?"

Siya guessed something bad has happened to him. Something worse than she could imagine.

"What's the matter, Sameer?"

"Ishika left me. She doesn't want me anymore. She broke the promise made to you. She forgot every moment we spent together."

While speaking, Sameer broke down. Tears were back in his eyes. Still, he tried to speak in his sobbing voice.

"Calm down, Sameer. Please don't cry. That will not change anything."

"Then what shall I do, if not cry?"

"Give me her phone number. I will talk to her."

"No, Siya. Please don't. I don't want you or anyone else to talk to her now."

"She broke her promise. What did she tell, anyway?"

"Ishika said that she wants someone who takes her out every weekend. Someone, who leaves his parents for her. Someone, who earns more than her and buys her expensive gifts. She insulted me by saying, 'I am just an insignificant artist and she earns a lot more than me'. Success, fame, and money have made her blind, Siya."

"Don't worry, Sameer. You will eventually forget her. Just keep yourself busy. Did you try contacting her after all this?"

"No. I deleted her phone number."

"Good. Don't even think of contacting her again."

"I am not going to her now. Anyway, I have decided something else."

"What?"

"I am going to marry a small-town girl. I have told my parents to search one for me."

"Don't take any decision in such a hurry."

"No. I have decided."

"Sameer, give yourself some time. And why specifically small-town girl?"

"Because she will value me more than Ishika?"

"What if she doesn't?"

"Then, I will accept my fate and live with her anyhow."

"Sameer, please. Think at least for once."

"No, Siya. I can't take my decision back. I want to discover, what destiny has in store for me."

"In that case, I cannot say anything. I hope your decision turns out to be right."

"I hope the same."

"Best of luck, Sameer."

"Thank you. I will talk to you later then."

"Ok. Bye."

"Bye, Siya."

Sameer took the day off. He wanted to spend some time alone locked in his apartment. He switched on the television to distract himself. He flipped through different music channels. But, adding to his grief, all were playing either romantic or sad songs. Those songs started to bring back memories even more. So, he switched off the television. He started scrolling his social media. But nothing interested him. He turned off his phone too. His eyes fell on the dining table and he remembered, he had kept breakfast there. He walked up to the table and took a bite of the food. The food had turned cold. So, he threw that food in the dustbin and stayed without breakfast.

Sameer was lying on his bed, trying to forget Ishika. But the more he tried to forget her, the more of their memories flashed back in his mind. He tried emptying his mind of her. But it is never easy to forget someone you love. He kept fighting his mind over Ishika's thoughts.

Days passed. Sameer still wasn't over Ishika. He still couldn't forget her. But at least, he didn't cry remembering her now. He had learned to cope with thoughts of her. He started to do well at his work again. He spent all day working. But at night, he couldn't escape her. He still saw her face when he closed his eyes.

After months of search, Sameer's parents finally found a girl, who was right for him. Also, she was according to

Sameer's told description, a small-town girl. Her name was Neha. She worked for an NGO in the small town of Sirohi.

Sameer agreed to meet her. On their first meeting, Sameer told Neha everything about him. His qualification, his job, his past relationship, and the reason for their break-up.

Neha accepted his past and him as he was. Also, she didn't want him to leave his parents. In her eyes, she had no respect for a boy who abandons his parents for a girl. She agreed to move in with him along with his parents. They decided to move to Delhi permanently, where Sameer worked, with his parents. Neha decided to leave her current NGO and join a new one there.

Neha and Sameer asked their parents to decide on a date as soon as possible for their wedding. They didn't want to prolong their marriage.

Sameer's parents consulted a priest and fixed the most recent date eligible for the wedding.

Sameer didn't want a high-profile wedding. So, he with Neha's agreement decided for a court marriage. Thus, the families had no preparations to do for the wedding. They just sat back and waited for the wedding day to arrive.

Eventually, the day arrived. Both families gathered in court and signed the papers and marriage certificate under the lawyer's guidance. Sameer and Neha garlanded each other and they were declared married.

Sameer and Neha celebrated the evening with their friends and distributed sweets to relatives and neighbors.

After a few days of their marriage, Sameer and Neha, along with his parents moved to Delhi permanently, selling their house in Udaipur.

Sameer managed his institute as before in Delhi. He did other works as he used to do. Neha joined an NGO, that focused on the education of orphan children. She too kept herself busy with her work like Sameer. She also managed her household work well. She never disrespected her in-laws or Sameer. She loved everyone and they all loved her too.

Sameer was now satisfied with his life. He had the work of his dream. He had loving parents. He had a supportive and sensible wife. He also had a recognition of his own. And, he didn't have any memories of Ishika. He demanded nothing more from his life. He just wished it to stay as it is and looked forward to becoming the best husband for Neha.

Which one will you choose, LOVE or FAME?

Printed by Libri Plureos GmbH in Hamburg, Germany